Mrs. Latimer Had a Fat Cat

*And Other Cozy
Mystery Poems*

Edited by Mary Ann Meussling
Published by Patricia Rockwell

For information, email Cozy Cat Press, cozycatpress@aol.com or visit our website at: www.cozycatpress.com

COZY CAT
P R E S S

ISBN: 978-1-946063-83-0
Printed in the United States of America

10 9 8 7 6 5 4 3 2 1

Dedicated to all lovers of cats, mysteries, and poetry

Foreword

In early 20   Cozy Cat Press announced a cozy
mystery P wished to enter regardless of age or
anyone e criteria were to write a poem or poems
locatinan three) about a mystery. At the deadline,
(no eceived 266 submissions from around the
w far more than we expected.

ext step involved selecting judges to choose the
of the entries to appear in an anthology of poems.
selected three judges—Jaimie Patterson, Melissa
Brooks, and Mario Sakran. In addition to ourselves, we
each read all of the entries and selected, blind to author
name, what we each considered to be the best. Of these
finalists, we chose first, second, and third place
winners who each received $100, $50, and $25,
respectively. You will find these three top winners and
all the other finalists' poems in the pages of this
anthology.

We wish to thank our talented designer and illustrator
who created the cover and the drawings for the top
three winners and several of the finalist poems.

We hope you enjoy this anthology and the wonderful
poems in it. Thank you for reading and supporting
these outstanding poets!

Mary Ann Meussling, Editor
Patricia Rockwell, Publisher

Table of Contents

Foreword

In early 2019, Cozy Cat Press announced a cozy mystery poetry contest. We opened our contest up to anyone who wished to enter regardless of age or location. The criteria were to write a poem or poems (no more than three) about a mystery. At the deadline, we had received 266 submissions from around the world—far more than we expected.

Our next step involved selecting judges to choose the best of the entries to appear in an anthology of poems. We selected three judges—Jaimie Patterson, Melissa Brooks, and Mario Sakran. In addition to ourselves, we each read all of the entries and selected, blind to author name, what we each considered to be the best. Of these finalists, we chose first, second, and third place winners who each received $100, $50, and $25, respectively. You will find these three top winners and all the other finalists' poems in the pages of this anthology.

We wish to thank our talented designer and illustrator who created the cover and the drawings for the top three winners and several of the finalist poems.

We hope you enjoy this anthology and the wonderful poems in it. Thank you for reading and supporting these outstanding poets!

Mary Ann Meussling, Editor
Patricia Rockwell, Publisher

Table of Contents

Bart J. Gilbertson, 1ˢᵗ Place Winner
Mrs. Latimer Had a Fat Cat

Bart currently lives in Idaho and is a father of two and grandfather of three. He has always had a love for poetry. He often recalls reciting poems with his father growing up, specifically "Two Pictures" by an unknown author, and "The Face upon the Barroom Floor" by John Henry Titus. He credits both for shaping his writing into what it is today.

Bart considers himself an average person just pursuing his dream. He is a voracious reader of fiction, no matter the genre. In his own writing, he works to put a good quality story on the shelf, and you can find many of his other published works on his Amazon page.

Bart has entered other poetry writing contests in the past, but this time, he really wanted to put his own stamp on 'stories that stick'. "Mrs. Latimer Had a Fat Cat" was inspired partly by older *Alfred Hitchcock Presents* episodes and the aforementioned poems his Dad used to share. He looks forward to reading all the poems in this anthology.

Finally, Bart would like to thank everyone who participated in the contest, everyone who's supported him over the years as he pursued his dream of being a published author, and you—the reader.

The Berlin Baker

By Janet Turner

They buried the Berlin baker yesterday—
full farinaceous honours and floral display,
a cob-shaped coffin and batons waved all
  the way.

In this great city he was born and bred.
He made his dough and now he's dead.
He was put in a pit o' local clay—
but that was what happened yesterday.

For it seems the baker's been seen around
by the head teacher in the school playground.
So the digger is out unearthing the mound.
And here comes the box—crumbs! It's
  dropped to the ground.

The top's toppled off and there's nothing inside.
Does the baker live or has he died?
Did he rise like his bread? I must decide,
though his death was definitely certified.

It will take a few days to find out the truth–
but I will—for I'm Berlin's invincible sleuth.

Janet Turner, 2nd Place Winner
The Berlin Baker

Janet is a retired University lecturer. She has three children who are grown up, and she now has more time for the writing she loves. However, she remembers that when her children were young, she would tell them countless stories and amuse them with poems made up on the spot. She now lives in the south of England with her husband. Janet holds a Diploma in Creative Writing from the Open University.

Janet has five self-published adult books—*Off the Rails, Legacy of Guilt, Jack's Sea, Missing Lucy* and *The Root of Evil*—all self-published with Amazon, and two more completed novellas that are waiting in the wings. Janet has also had non-fiction and poetry published in magazines and anthologies and a short story published by Spine and Page.

She has been writing seriously for about four years and became a member of Southampton Writing Buddies, enjoying discussions of her own and other members' work. Although she began by writing adult books, Janet is beginning to write stories for children and more poetry.

When not writing, Janet enjoys meeting with her family, walking, gardening, reading and playing croquet.

The Tea Is Cold

By Audrey Xuan

She sits warm in the corduroy chair,
The blanket on her lap guarding her from
  the world.
Her eyes tick across the page,
Pendulum-ing from line to line.
She sips quietly,
The near-boiling liquid sending heat down
  her body and into her soul.
On the other side of the glass,
Thunder roars like some strange beast.
She struggles to keep her mind on the book,
But feels herself being drawn away.
Though she could've sworn she closed the window,
There's a breeze and she feels the cool
  touch of water on her skin.
Frantic,
She rushes to the closet.
As the heavy-booted footsteps creep down the hallway,
She holds her breath.
Even the slightest sound or tiniest
  movement will give her away,
But she's running out of air and her lungs
  are screaming at her and her heart is furious.
The shadow approaches the slatted door,
Blocking the moonlight that falls across her face.
She knows how this will end,
She's read mystery novels.
When they find her,
The tea is cold.

Audrey Xuan, 3rd Place Winner
The Tea Is Cold

Audrey is an 18-year-old student and writer. She began writing when she was little, composing songs and poems for her family and friends. Though she's lived across Canada, she is proud to call Toronto home. Her upcoming projects include a road trip novel and a musical screenplay.

She's an editor at *Genius*, a music website, where she founded the Indie Monday initiative to promote independent and alternative musicians. Audrey also serves on her local library's youth editorial board. In her free time, she enjoys cooking and baking, thrift-shopping, watching *The Office*, and playing video games.

Audrey is fascinated by anything at the intersection of art, media, and technology, including film, photography, gaming, and graphic design. After university, she plans on attending college or film school to achieve her dream of becoming a writer-director.

Someone
By Claire Buss

Someone has eaten the last biscuit
Without permission and in blatant
  disregard of the rules
All that is left are miniscule crumbs
But there is enough evidence to follow the clues

Suspect number one is the husband
He grooms his moustache nervously
Blatant denial is marred by his darting gaze
Looking anywhere but at me

The children are brought in for questioning
The youngest seems very confused
Toddler demands for biscuit, biscuit, biscuit
And my line of enquiry swiftly breaks down

I consult the theft timeline minutely
Determining who else was at the scene of
  the crime
The mother-in-law was away that day
The pool of suspects has run dry

Cross examination and lie detection tests complete
No-one is changing their story
I boil the kettle in utter frustration
It's time for a cup of tea

It feels like forever since I last had a beverage

It was at least a quarter past nine
I remember it clearly
The last biscuit…

Had

Been

… Mine!

The Unwritten Stanza

By Diane Callahan

The butcher's wife went missing
on a skin-melting summer day,
and the whole town sizzled
with stories and speculation:
Oh, what a tragedy for such a woman
to be gone, lost, kidnapped
—dead?

A curious poet passing through
thought this stranger's story rather odd,
and because her own muse
had gone missing, too,
she tapped her chin and set to work
to find the butcher's wife.

When the poet went door to door,
the townspeople squeezed
out a solitary tear—maybe even two!—
for this poor angel who had flown away.
But behind closed doors,
smiles bloomed.

The not-quite-widowed butcher
stood in his shop among the stench of flesh
and wiped sticky sweat from his brow,
for which he blamed the August heat.
He told the poet that his wife had stormed
into the street when he had refused
to waste his latest boon so she could see

the bustling city beyond their quiet town,
where the women wore furs instead of cotton
and the men smoked cigars instead of meats.
But the money went missing with his sweet.

The poet left him to his cleaver,
and with each *slice slice slice*
the butcher wished it had been
the fingers
of that spoiled thief instead.

The book club vice president—
well, acting president, now that the butcher's wife
had so tragically disappeared—last saw
her frizzy-haired friend at the town library.
She told the poet they had, admittedly,
quarreled, perhaps a little loudly,
about whether to read an Austen or Brontë next.
For the butcher's wife had turned up her nose
at every book she chose, hungering
instead for harsher tales of murder and woe.
That woman had always loved her Poe.

The poet left her to her heavy tomes,
and with each *rip rip rip*
of the turning pages in her hands,
the vice president wished it had been
the nose
of that stupid snob instead.

The almost-retired gardener
tended the front flowerbeds,
white gardenias shining in the sun,

their perfume strong enough to mask any odor.
He told the poet that he and the butcher's wife
had once been the best of friends, but
he took a vow of silence
whenever she stood within listening ear
after she had smeared across the town
that he preferred the look of men.
He never entrusted her with secrets again.

The poet left him to his shears
and with each *snip snip snip*
the gardener wished it had been
the tongue
of that nasty gossip instead.

But their wishes died with the leaves
when the butcher's wife breezed back home
alive, greeting them all in her new furs,
which must've cost an arm and a leg.

She rhapsodized on and on about the city's
vivacious lights and how sad the town's drab
brick seemed to her feet, which were adorned
with brand new heels of highest fashion.
With the story clear, the poet's muse returned,
though the final stanza remained unwritten.

The robbed widower caressed his cleaver,
the new book club president hugged her heavy tomes,
the now-retired gardener snatched his shears,
and every single eye twinkled alike:
the next time the butcher's wife disappeared
they'd make sure she did it right.

Clean Getaway

By Haowen Fang

A dry autumn evening
A warm and cozy night
Slowly, slowly pulling up
A red luxury sedan

Chrome against the backdrop
Waning sun and waxing moon
Four figures, walking through
Barred doors and locked windows
As the last groundskeeper leaves

Strolling through empty hallways
They pick, choose and peruse
Paintings, jewelry, baubles, gems
No alarms sound, no sirens

Maneuvering between
Patrolling security
Unblinking cameras
Slithering under display
cases, between sculptures
Escaping before dawn break

Detectives were puzzled
No motion sensors troubled
The thieves circled the guards as
They claimed their spoils of war
And slipped away covertly

"Locks were undisturbed" said the
Trenchcoated detective
His hand in his scruffy hair
"There's no trace of entry
aside from 'a car was here!'"
Released from questioning
The groundskeeper listens in
Smiles, patting his pocket
His share of the prize within

Nearing Venice

By Kevan Taplin

Into the snake skin sky,
the toe-nail moon crept.

On a night of stillness.
Soft sounds sneaked across the landscape.

We met on the bridge in secret
and I wept into the lagoon.

Silent Voices

By Suvi Hollenbach

Doors blocking us from anything we might soon
  explore,
My son and I walked up the old creaky stair floors.
A Victorian house on a mysterious new land,
With cobwebs brushing up against my hands.

Night fell fast as stars struggled to glow,
Leaves rustled away from the winds mighty blow.
Slam!
A door was shut with someone inside,
No one was there except for my imaginative mind.

Morning finally came,
And my son rushed in calling my name.
"Mom…Mom!"
He said, "I need money for the trip to the mall."
I told him, "Okay, just be back before nightfall."

The phone was ringing as I quickly picked up,
Only static was there so swiftly I hung up.
I looked to my left as I thought I heard a shut,
My bookcase was moved from its dusty old rut.

Nothing was there, like a secret old door,
So I got to thinking more and more.
'What if the noise were not on my level,
But something lurking below sea level?'

I went back to that dusty old rut,
And under the rug was a trap door shut.
I opened and crawled with shivers down my spine,
Then I saw the telephone line.

I pushed the redial,
And waited for a while.
Until above I heard that awful sounding thing,
Ring...Ring...Ring.

Someone picked up as I held it against my ear,
Only static was heard as I began to fear.
'Someone unknown is walking alone,
For some reason picking up my phone.'

I bolted upstairs with nothing in thought,
And there he stood not even in shock.
My ex-husband stood with a malicious smile,
Thinking he could take my boy for a while.

The cops were on their way thanks to the phone below,
But that was something he did not know.
I talked and talked to try and stall the time, then
Bam! A cop managed to break inside.

I held my boy as all was resolved,
'Thank goodness this case did not go unsolved.'
We walked back up the old creaky stairs,
Hoping for no more living nightmares.

Missing Person

By Ella Wilson

Spilt coffee soaked the side table,
Jazmine wound her long grey tail around my ankle,
Bore a sorrowful glance from slanted blue eyes,
As if to say,
She misses her.

The uncertainty is what scares me the most,
A million scenarios,
Running through my head,
Is she still out there?
IS she coming home?

They looked everywhere,
The police,
But they can't confirm she's gone,
Until they know for sure,
Six months I've waited.

Halloween tomorrow,
My sister and I would carve a pumpkin every year,
Put it on the doorstep and giggle at grown men dressed
  as spiders,
Little dogs with dresses,
Would seem silly—doing it alone.

Up in the Air
By Hannah Lashyro

The bright August moon is
up in the air

Much like the impending
air the future of a
newlywed couple

All of it is up in the air

Table set for two, a
quaint cabin in the woods

Candles and gaudy
silverware and facades

Embellish the linen on
the table in the air

After that bright August moon
slinks down behind itself

The candles are out
Her candle is out

Snubbed out without
much of a care in
the world

Her neck is decorated
In ruby red, from a
distance the blood seems
like precious gems

He is nowhere to
be seen, the back
window is cracked

It was all up in the
air, and he with it.

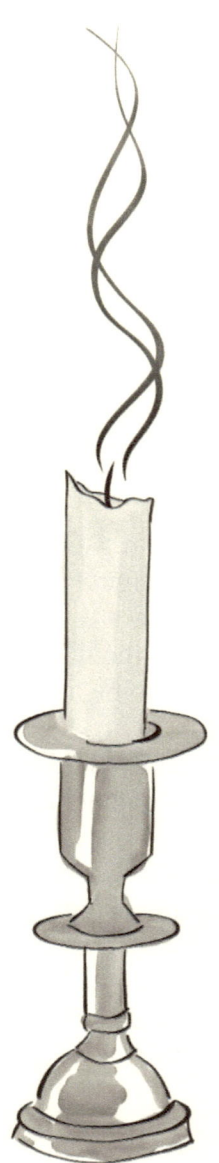

The Strange Disappearance of Lila Raz

By Ella Sheridan

I saw a man come searching
He asked for Lila Raz
They claim they have not seen her
He's sure that someone has

He was a very odd man
No hair upon his head
I know I saw his twisted face
That night that Lila fled

That night the air was frozen
I snuck in through the back
I curled up upon her rug
And readied for a nap

Snoozing on my patch of warmth
(Though Lila never knew)
She took her coat, her hat, her bag
And out the door she flew

Woken in a frightened state
Spooked by Lila's racket
I'm sure she did not notice when
A note fell from her jacket

I yawned and rose to my feet
The abandoned thing beckoned

It looked completely ordinary
But changed my life that second
SMASH!
Something broke through the window
CRASH!
It exploded in flames

I run toward the back door
The letter in my teeth
But that chance was shut and bolted
The fire hissed and seethed

Leaping through the hungry waif
I made a final pass
But frightfully misjudged my jump
And caught on broken glass

It was then I saw him
A demon in the darkness
His face was split in grinning
His eyes putrid, heartless

I stole away in silence
Far away from the flames
Once the fire was doused and drowned
I returned to what remained

I crept beneath the rubble
And found a blackened ring
A voice rang out that turned me cold
And caused my cut to sting

"Was the body found?" It said

And a new voice replied
"No, the house was empty, sir"
The odd man stopped mid stride

"So you think she has escaped?"
The new voice creased his brow
"I think it's good they made it out"
The truth dawned on him now

But doubt flits across his face
He's feared this for some time
Perhaps if I bring the answer he needs
Then he will bring me mine

I rush to get the letter
Before the new man leaves
Reaching in to my hiding place
I pull it from the eaves

It was then that I heard it
That familiar sound
From a window right above me
My hope leapt up unbound

I nudged the window open
On seeing me she cried
"Oh, you poor thing," she said sadly
"You're all burnt up the side!"

I placed the letter in her lap
Lila laughs "Just what we need!"
She tossed me some fish from her plate
And said, "Hear that? We're free."

The History of Mystery

By Elizabeth Horrocks

Let us examine the history of Mystery:
the first of the brood is perhaps Edwin Drood.
Unfinished, and so a double conundrum,
but lively, as Dickens just doesn't do humdrum.

Then cross the Atlantic for E. Allan Poe:
His C. Auguste Dupin's the first detective, you know.
The Rue Morgue Murders and the Purloined Letter…
The first the more famous, the second, perhaps better.

The Mystery writer with followers most loyal
for over a century is A. Conan Doyle.
Sherlock Holmes is quite peerless and so often has
  been
reincarnated by actors on stage and screen.

We move then to what's known as The Golden Age,
And still famous writers now come on the stage.
In Britain there's a whole lot of women who shine—
Christie, Sayers, or Marsh, they're all of them fine.

In the States it was darker, more violent, gritty,
with Chandler and Hammett and the crimes of the city.
Marlowe and Spade are their heroes of choice.
Quite unlike Miss Marple, a less strident voice.

And now we are coming to more recent times,
when there's been a proliferation of crimes.

All recorded by R. Hill (that's Dalziel and Pascoe)
Or Rankin in Edinburgh, or Mina in Glasgow.

Paretsky and Grafton or the fine J.D. Robb,
Louise Penny, McDearmid, all do a great job.
McCall Smith has used an exotic location—
in Botswana, where Ladies pursue this vocation.

So let us all cheer for this rich, varied history
of writers of crime, of murder and mystery.
Let's drink to the authors who continue to floor us,
and raise loud our voices in a great "Thank you"
 chorus.

Lost in Transmission
By Anna-Maria Mazy

Click and send
It is that simple
My words and wishes, deepest thoughts
And virtual love
For you go out.
It is always so—
We write and send out
Greetings, wishes
Dreams
Through cyberspace
And sending wait for answer;
And wait in silence.

Perhaps you are busy
Since there is no quick reply
Perhaps you are not there
Since nightfall brings no word
And time moves on
Swifter than lightning…
Sending again I wonder and ask
Where you are
And my message is just to cry out
To say, "Hey, are you there?
Are you there?"

I am still here
Still waiting
Still waiting for a reply
And knowing there is a good answer
Trusting for an answer, a reason
For the silence
I wait.
And perhaps at last you will respond:
Telling me of this and that
All the myriad reasons and excuses
And oh so good explanations

And perhaps I will have word:
That I will never have an answer
That some great upheaval broke the world
And you are gone.

And perhaps
More likely I will never hear
And never know if you are still living or dead
Or just gone from where I wait
In the ghosted spaces of the internet
Where memory lasts as long as time.

And the words I sent to you are gone too
Vanished with that final click
Somewhere in the wired unwired web
Weaving us all together
And yet so far apart
That a million mysteries
Fall in the spaces between
The sender and the reply.

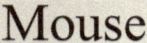

Mouse
By Thomas Ellison

Awake, animal
with the smooth shell,
like a large dry pebble,

when the hand rests
on top, like a caress,
you fit like a glove.

You like to be pressed
with tenderness,
you have a right and a left,

the beginnings of a horn,
like a notched wheel,
between your glued eyes.

In your mouth you hold your tail,
twisted of gold and silver,
it runs beyond the borders,

awake, and we will dance,
and the arrow will dance
beyond the borders.

Stacy's Poem

By Anastasia Ifenedo

As silent as the heavens
A figure sat in the tavern
In a dark red hood
Shrouding a calculating look

How funny, I didn't see
When it rose and followed me
Down the cobbled streets
Through the red, red beets

It was a resounding clang
On my head, like a bang
That awakened my sense
To its formidable presence

And I fell upon the soil
My fluids staining the farmer's toil
I was given the last gift
As my eyes I did lift

And they met dark steel
That and the royal seal
The Prince murdered me
Or was it really he?

Whodunnit?

By Kayleen Denis

The car flipped and flipped and flipped.
It hit the ground and it rolled.
The glass shattered and the air bags deployed.

Miraculously and very fortunately not a single soul
    was hurt.
Yes, I said soul.
Bodies were damaged.

Lungs punctured.
Femurs fractured.
And ribs shattered.

During interviews the victims were asked what
    happened.
Whodunnit?
Where was it?

The driver said that it was a dark night and his tail
    lights weren't on
He must've driven into a deer
The passenger said she doesn't know what happened.
It was cold the road might have been slick.
Just like humans cars can slip.

But to slip that far into the air there must've been
something there.
Someone?

Luckily for the victims we can see what was going on
The highway had a new video system.
In the playback we see something that should be in the
  books

One second she's there and the next
poof.

An Interrogation

By Angelica Esquivel

"You're in danger,"
I tell the man as he sits, sweating
beneath the bright fluorescent lights.
His eyes are wet with tears.

The bodies of two of his colleagues
have been discovered, clean kills in
tidy law offices, spacious views of the city.

"You're likely the murderer's next target," I say.
"Why would someone want to kill you?"
He dabs his forehead with a handkerchief.

Tells a story about a disgruntled former client.
I lay out the evidence on the dingy metal table: a
pistol with a silencer, no fingerprints.

A cigarette butt, the ring it burned into the carpet.
A secretary called in sick and an airtight alibi.
The man's hands shake. He folds them into his lap. He
is afraid,

But of what? I don't have an answer. Death and
captivity, To many, these are the same thing.

Panic

By Mark Henderson

A man in a wheelchair opens the door to the stairs.
Stairs look like sawblades when seen from the side.
A blade on its side is a line drawn on paper.
Every surface is a line
                    coming for us all.

That's how Sonny's mind worked alright: always
  connecting
things, anxiously and obsessively, to
the most panic-inducing conclusions. No one
freaked out at a wheelchair-bound
                    man taking the stairs?

What would've made him take such a chance? To
  tempt Fate
like that? Was he faking his condition?
He couldn't fake levitation, that was for sure.
Gravity doesn't take breaks.
                    Neither does Sonny.

Sonny Sachs, that is. Private investigator.
His ringtone was even a saxophone—
smoky, sultry, and anticipating dames in
distress. But no dames came. No
                    young ones, anyway.

It was an old one, after all, who'd come to him,
telling him of the "tragic accident."
A great-grandmother, ignored just enough by her

family to see the door
                    close on the rear wheels.

A man in a wheelchair opens the door to the stairs.
Stairs look like sawblades when seen from the side.
A blade on its side is a line drawn on paper.
Every surface is a line
                    coming for us all.

He'd written it down again. Intuition, you
might call it. A feeling that something worse
than the fall was going to happen, that no one
would see coming. You have to
                    figure in chaos.

As it turns out, the man in the wheelchair had it in
for Sonny; he was tired of all his damned muttering—
his endless connecting of the unconnected—
while playing happy boy scout
                    to the handicapped.

Amazing that a man who'd gotten the news from his
doctor that he had only weeks to live
would need further reason for suicide. Sonny
could drive you crazy enough
                    to kill him *and* you.

So the bomb went off at the bottom of the stairs, where
Sonny was investigating. It was
full of razors and index cards. It was mostly
the cards that killed Sonny. On
                    each one was written:

A man in a wheelchair opens the door to the stairs.
Stairs look like sawblades when seen from the side.
A blade on its side is a line drawn on paper.
Every surface is a line
                    coming for us all.

Mystery Haiku

By Ben Ditmars

what was in school lunch,
yesterday? was it real food?
or an alien?

i think i ate an
alien! UGH! WHERE IS THE
SOAP!? I need some soap!

get me the soap, *please*.
or a jug of clean water…
it might be over.

tell my mom i love
her, but i ate an alien…
she can't be near me.

i'm running away
to a place for kids who might
invade the planet

if I start puking
green goo, just stab it with a
pencil—i'll be fine.

Crabby Crenshaw's Demise
By Jenny Burr

The day began in the usual way with Lindsey opening
her store,
Treasured Again, a shop of items, to be loved by others
once more.

Completing her walkabout within, she stepped out of
the shop's back door.
On the deck she spotted someone in a chair, yet there
was something more

Tasking herself to check it out she stepped onto the
deck, then stopped
It was Crabby Crenshaw, the retired teacher, in the
chair, heavily flopped.

Cold to the touch, very pale too, Lindsey dug out her
phone and dialed.
A short time later, Officer Do Little, arrived and he
smiled.
.

"Why did you do it?" he accused and pierced her with
his gaze.
"I didn't," said Lindsey, "I found her," returning a
similar gaze.

Solve the crime to prove her innocence is precisely
what she would do
And she was certain that she would be able to locate a
suspect or two.

'

Before Do Little had arrived she had used her phone to snap pics,
Mud on the deck, and on Crabby's shoes, her hair with tiny sticks.

Glasses askew, scrapes on her arms and a typed note which read,
"To be or not to be? That is the question." The answer is to be dead.

People who knew Crabby, recognized her favorite Shakespearian quote,
An indication the suspect also knew when they fabricated the note.

"I declare it a suicide," said Do Little, "The note says it all."
The medical team arrived then Do Little left to answer a call.

Not surprised at his snap decision, Lindsey glanced at the scene once more.
Walking to the edge of the deck, something glittered near the shed door.

Stepping off the deck, she leaned down closer to examine her newest find.
Grasping the item with a tissue from her pocket, thoughts on her mind.

Crabby never wore jewelry, so the bracelet was a definite clue.

She placed it into her pocket. It was then that Lindsey knew.

The typed note, was the first mistake; Crabby despised the digital age,
Only accepting handwritten work from her students, pen upon the page.

Crabby had taught many students but would any have done this deed?
What about Crabby's siblings or friends, wanting her death to speed?

Who had the most to gain? Lindsey pondered, as she turned to go inside.
Who had a reason to be free of Crabby and to hide murder as suicide?

Lindsey entered the store's back door, leaving the marked crime scene.
Only office work today because of Do Little's investigative team.

Her office allowed a perfect view of where Crabby met her demise.
And perhaps a place of return for the suspect was Lindsey's surmise.

To look for a bracelet? To confirm their success? Or delight in their gain?
Lindsey determined to work at her desk and observe what might explain.

Crabby was a miserable person, but she lived for every day.
Criticizing energized her, she never let anyone get in her way.

In her view, Crabby was right and that was all that mattered.
But a daily dose of Crabby, might make a person feel battered.

Townsfolk wandered past, some paused to point and stare.
Others chatted with the team in hopes of being more aware.

When the team departed, fewer people stopped by
Later that afternoon, two people came by to spy.

Then, they entered the scene, moving the dirt with their feet.
Sending a text to Do Little, Lindsey went out, to greet.

The two acting strangely were Kent and Kelly, the Crenshaw twins.
Searching for the lost bracelet? Or perhaps hiding clues within?

"Yesterday we walked through the woods," said Kent.
"Kelly lost something."
Kelly nodded from Kent to Lindsey, as they heard a cell phone ring.

Do Little rounded the corner as Lindsey displayed the bracelet.

"Where did you find it?" asked Kent. Lindsey pointed to the spot.

"What's going on?" Do Little asked. So, Lindsey explained her thought.

"The twins likely gave Crabby sleeping pills and took her for a walk

Through the woods, to my store, hoping not to be caught.

They left Crabby to sleep to her death, but the plan was all for naught."

Modern Malice
By Natalia Pelayo

Mass market mystery maven
Mulls multiple murders.
Motive, motive, motive
Meets modern malice.

Tea Time Murder
By Natalia Pelayo

Lipstick-stained teacup
in the killer's favorite pink shade.
Solves the cold case.

Follow the Arrows

By Ashley Baum

follow the arrows
   scratched into the cold pavement
      all the signs will lead you back to her
         follow the arrows
            deep red streaks across the cracked
concrete
you want to find her, don't you?
follow the arrows
they're everywhere, just look
every arrow points you closer and closer
follow the arrows
she's still breathing…breathing…
unless you don't find all the clues
follow the arrows
look around look around
isn't it so…obvious
follow the arrows
oh, there we go, now we're thinking
you can almost sense her silent screams
follow the arrows
faster now, pick up the pace
she can't afford to wait
follow the arrows
I'm giving you all the answers!
don't you just adore my little game?
follow the arrows
almost there, you're so close
I can see you
follow the arrows

oh no, an empty room…
but where did she go?
follow the arrows

A Night at a B&B in Colorado

By Pam Reese

The crying woke them.
"Who is it?"
"Not the kids."
The crying continued.
"It's not them."
"It's outside."
The crying continued.
"It's cats."
"Siamese cats."
The crying diminished. Silence.
They closed their eyes to sleep.
"CAROLINE"S OKAY!"
A craggy voice whispered beside the bed.
Eyes flew open.
No one there. Silence…
At breakfast, they asked:
"Who is Caroline?"
"Many have asked," she answered, "but we do not
know.
This house was once
An asylum.
Maybe Caroline lived here.
Maybe Caroline lived here."

Windshield Wipers

By Alexis Reder

They lay curled on the pavement,
swaddled in the gold glowing blanket
draped from the headlights.
In the folds of luminance, the red
on their clothes glared at me
through the window.
My fingers wrung the leathered wheel,
choking in hate
for either myself
or them in the road,
yet pulling it close to my chest
for some kind of block
to my leaving heart,
taunted by the beating windshield.

If it weren't for the wipers,
I could just let the figure drown in
    raindrops,
giving myself time to understand
what happened…
if I struck the gas pedal by mishap or malice.
            But they kept pulsing
            and renewing
            the image presented
            across the ground,
            moaning again and again,
            as if grieving the word
                        "look…
                    look…
                look…"

The Woman

*By Susan Butle*r

An empty house
An open door
No one home
Forever more
Where did she go?
From whence
she came?
No one left
Her home to claim
No husband, children,
father or mother
No friends
or nosy neighbors
to bother
She lived alone
And alone was fine
She left with one
Not unlike her kind
No one saw him
Enter or leave
No sign of struggle
No vandals or thieves
　　　He left
　　　with
　　　nothing
　　　Save one
　　　thing
　　　—The woman

Crimson Kiss

By Shelby Yarchin

His stare reminded her of a sad clown painted.
Lips drawn the color of a ripened apple, bruised and
  battered.
A cup of coffee lightened with creamer sat in front of
him, the mug cracked.
It dripped, dripped, dripped scalding liquid onto a tile
  table.
He held a newspaper—two days old, the headline
  screaming

MURDER IN THE CITY!

He ordered a scone the next day.

It sat on the royal blue paper napkin until it bled
  through.
The strawberry jam oozed past flaky crust and stained
  the table red.
The mug rested without a crack, coffee a darkened
  black.
The paper was folded, but she could still read in big,
  bold letters

KILLER STRIKES AGAIN!

The paint was applied with less precision the day after.
His smile dripped with a darkened brown, eyes blue
  diamonds.
The scone was left untouched dropping flakes of pastry

like snow.

He raised the mug to his lips, leaving a kiss of crimson
behind.

Yellowed glasses reflected the simple text—hot
pressed, fresh

CITY LEFT IN TERROR!

He had wiped away most of the makeup.

Little white flecks of paint decorated his cheeks in
freckles.

Blue rimmed his sickly stare and crimson cracked lips.

Coffee left untouched until cold and untainted.

Dirt rimmed nails creased another headlining story.

DNA EVIDENCE FOUND. KILLER CAUGHT?

The man with a painted face left a vacant seat

Black coffee sat at the bottom of a drip, solidifying.

Colored cobalt prints reflected against the tile in small
spirals

He had forgotten to wipe them away.

A paper rested on the diner's counter—untouched,
bleeding ink.

KILLER CAUGHT!

Death Is a Master of Art

By Kristal Jonasen

Her spilled blood sparkled like rubies in the moonlight
Her hair was a black river beneath her body
Body exquisite,
Body rigid in death,
Death is always pretty, I thought as I examined her,
Death is a master of art,
"Art, do we have any leads?" I asked
Art turned toward me and said, "No."
No leads,
No motive, except the obvious—
Obvious, even in death, was her beauty
Obvious, even in death, was her terror—
Terror had stretched her mouth wide,
Terror had kept her eyes open, unseeing,
Unseeing as the river of her blood,
Unseeing as a fish dragged to shore, eyes milky-white;
Milky-white, her skin shone bright beneath the moon,
Milky-white, her eyes stared,
Stared at nothing,
Stared at everything,
Everything about this death shouted, 'premeditated',
Everything shouted, 'serial killer',
Killer on the loose,
Killer who always left,
Left a single rose, red, nestled within the victim's
  bosom,
Left the body poised,
Poised beneath the billowing arms of a willow tree,

Poised within the stifling confines of a cemetery,
Cemeteries stunk of death and rot,
Cemeteries welcomed both the dead and the living,
Living must have been hard on her, I thought,
Living had given her calloused hands,
Hands that held slender fingers, clasped around
  nothing,
Hands that spoke of hard work,
"Work this as a serial," I said. Art nodded.
Work was the detective's middle name.
"Name?" I asked, knowing it would be Jane Doe,
Names of this particular serial's victims were
  unknown,
Unknown despite all their beauty,
"Unknown," said Art, as always, and I knew,

Knew that, if Art remained in charge, we would never
  know,
Knew that we would work this case like we had all the
others,
Others who had died,
Others who had been poised so pretty,
Pretty in death,
Pretty as posies,
Posies left on her resting place by me, by the guilty,
Posies left on her grave by Art...
Art
Guilty

In Cold Blood

By Karla Dearsley

They found the body when the snow melted.
A blizzard five days earlier had piled it high into a bank
For kids to slide down,
Or make angel stars.
The man lay curled up on his side,
As if asleep.
Dubbed "John Doe" by the police,
But the woman watching—
Eyes shaded by a hat,
Collar pulled high,
Hands thrust in pockets—
Knew his name was Kit Maguire.
She had been his secretary—
P.A. to the P.I.—now she's the boss.
Her first case would be his last.
A redhead dumped the bag with his belongings
At the office.
Said she was his wife—
Cold as stone and hard as ice—
"Tell him that I never loved him.
Tell him not to bother coming back."
He saw the bag—no need to say more.
She'd left him singing to a bottle—
He'd done it many times before.

The blizzard came the night he vanished
When he was staking out a suspect.
She found the photos later in a desk drawer

Of a woman in flagranté.
With hot red hair that left no doubt,
The suspect was his wife.
The woman knew there'd be no sign
Of violence–only misadventure,
But murder comes in many guises.
His wife had used the cruelest weapon—
Words that cut him like the east wind.
The cause of death?
A frozen heart.

A Cinquain for Murder
By Loralee Petersen

Mystery
Lies, secrets
End in death
A puzzle to solve
Whodunnit

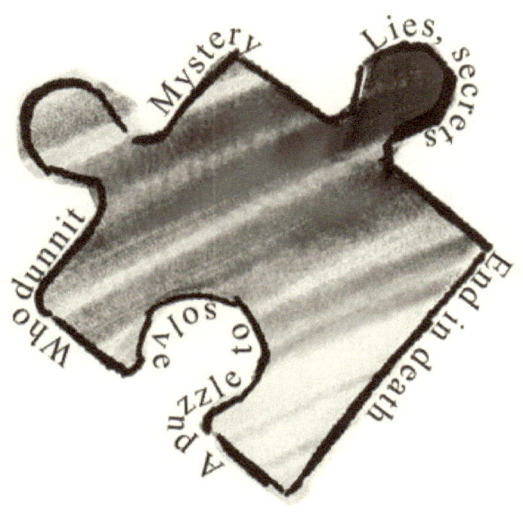

How Death Comes
By Lindsey Keller

per a palm with splayed fingers,
per a live nerve, per birds
breaking their wings in spite,
per knuckled cheeks, tremors,
topography of organs.
per shredded paper napkins
that dust your feet, per spines,
per papier-maché ripping thick
and wet, a compass rose
bud blistering open.
per fire, smoke.
per smoke, a fire.
per electric collars with unknown fences,
tear gas grenades, per glinting
edges of staircase, grit tooth whistling.
per boozy firemen stacking themselves
upon each other for kindling.
per the wilted umbilical cord
on your old body, fraying,
per faulty cardiac sprinklers,
a flinch of prostration,
a magnifying glass used for shade.
per hushed air taken as paper-bag breathing,
hagiography taken for history.

The Faint Glow
By Tessa-Mae Little

The faint glow of the moon struggles to pierce through
  the smog,
And the face of the clock is dimly illuminated.
Revealing half past midnight.
Detective Jem Bowen is slumped against the dank
  limestone. A watchdog.

Across the way, through the hustle and bustle, the
  lovely Lady Primrose sits with fright.
Tonight, she will be kidnapped, so between sips of hot
  chamomile she shivers with fear.
Jem watches her through the window intently. A trap
  set, but her upset is a sad sight.

Suddenly, and swiftly, a malicious character prances
  beneath her window to peer.
Detective Jem, quick with intuition, advances across
  the cobble stone in pursuit.
The slinky figure whips his head back at Jem, through
  the shadows, with a menacing jeer.

Taking off in haste, weaving through the crowd,
  splashing through the mud with a large boot.
Jem flaps his coat, to keep up with his pace. This
  criminal too important to lose.
For he is the nefarious gem thief, the swarthy lady
  killer. He claims his loot.

His face plastered on the front of every paper. High

profile news.
Jem's job relies on this capture. He plans to expose.
In the middle of the chase. Jem stared at the man,
  puzzled, it felt like a ruse.

Doubling back, and quickly this time, Jem advanced
  toward the house of the Lady Primrose
For he had been made a fool. How could it have
  slipped past? He peers in the window.
Stiff as board, draped on the carpet, she begins the
  process to decompose.

The Elephant Lady
By Savannah Kimble

I was babysitting at the Fosters' house,
the day she walked on by.
She waved at little Freddy
and he ducked behind me, so shy.
"Who was that?" he whispered quick,
underneath his breath.
I stared in shock before I said,
"Dear old Miss Elizabeth?"
He nodded up with eyes so wide,
as the old lady passed by like a queen.
"Well, she's the Elephant Lady, of course—the best
detective this town's ever seen!"
His brow furrowed in confusion
as he stared at the distance where she'd shrunk.
"But if they call her that…
why doesn't she have a trunk?"
I laughed aloud at his child's mind,
happiness honking like a horn.
"If you promise to listen,
I'll tell you a story from before you were born.
Once, there was a circus
that rolled into the town,
and people came from far and wide
to see the dancing clowns.
Like magic it came, with colors so bright,
with jugglers and giraffes too,
with tigers, and with lions,
—it was really nearly a zoo!

But the best beast of all
was an elephant so large…
even in the Big Top,
he looked like a barge!
The circus brought joy,
all our worries banished,
and then one day,
the elephant vanished!
They awoke one fine morn
to feed him his hay,
only to discover
that he had gone away!
No one knew how it happened,
no one guessed his scheme,
and so no one could know
how he could be redeemed.
We searched high and low,
checked every cave,
yet no one could find him,
and the matter grew grave.
Weeks went by
with nary a hint,
no hide nor hair,
no elephant print.
And finally Miss Elizabeth,
after the circus had left,
stepped into the spotlight
with deduction skills deft.
She lived alone,
and knew the elephant's lonely mind.
She knew that after escape,
he would search out his own kind.
They found him above the interstate,

with a peanut billboard,
caressing his fellow pachyderm
with a love that could not be ignored.
And so dear Miss Elizabeth
found her companion at last.
He lived with her for many years,
until finally in peace, he passed.
Miss Elizabeth, of course,
also found fame,
and as the Elephant Lady,
she knows visitors, love, and acclaim."

Small Prints, Big Claws
By Nancy Clark

When penniless Franny vanished one day,
her friends never dreamed she went away
to secretly harass her estranged great-aunt.
Miss Mabel Blunt was known to flaunt
her jewels, diamonds, emeralds, pearls,
in collars for cats she called 'her wee girls.'
She'd shot to fame down in Tennessee
singing her songs at the Grand Old Opry.
The ballads she wrote turned solid gold,
making a fortune each time one was sold.
When Fran saw an interview with Mabel
saying cats were her heirs on national cable,
she swore she'd get into the old girl's will
and never again dodge an overdue bill.
Scraping together enough for a round-trip flight,
Fran went to the mansion geared up for a fight.
When she referred to the genes they shared,
her great-aunt merely snorted and stared,
saying bad blood would never get her wealth.

Unable to bend her, Fran turned to stealth.
She was just removing a cat's bejeweled collar
when Great-aunt Mabel let out a furious holler.
Franny jumped up as the cat's claws drew blood
and throttled Mabel, who fell with a thud.
Franny ran half a mile before calling an Uber
and flew back home certain that nobody knew her
connection to Mabel so they'd never guess

and the murder would stay a mysterious mess.
But where there's a will there's more than one way
to skin a cat when proving there's been foul play.
Not only did security cameras catch Fran in the act,
but her DNA turned up on the claws of the cat.

Suspicion
By Mary E. Koppel

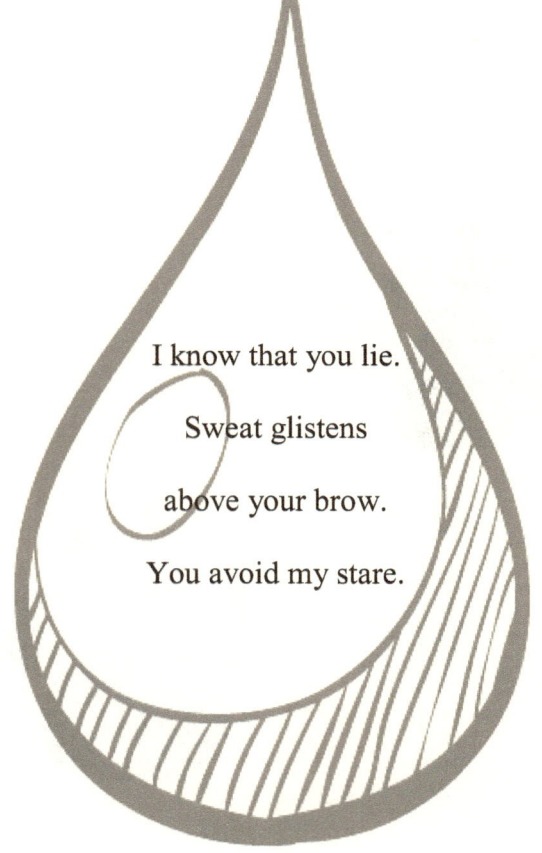

I know that you lie.

Sweat glistens

above your brow.

You avoid my stare.

Mercury
By Ana Vidosavljevic

The mercury ran though her.
Its sinister nature damaged her.
Unrepairable, mutilated, butchered.
She was abandoned. Forever.
No return to the normal state.
No light at the end of the tunnel.
She was breathing the poison from the painting for
many years.
Latex paint, all over that masterpiece.
That masterpiece was a gift from him.
What had he done?
Why?
No tomorrow waited for her.
Was it a thin line between love and hate?
He would find her.
Breathless, immobile.
And he would get rid of her body.
Wait…
Not yet…
She was still moving.
She grabbed the phone receiver.
911.

Full Moon
By Sandra James

in the dead of night
a sombre full moon
peeps through my curtain
and spies me in bed
restless, awake
unable to sleep—
a creak on the stairs
footsteps I hear
I shiver
I cower…I tremble with fear
afraid to call out…
Who is out there?
the hoot of an owl
the howl of a dog
the cat flap is swinging
back and forth in the wind
a dark shadow slinks
across the face of the moon
crone on her broomstick
and an evil black cat…with eyes glowing red
he hisses
she cackles
I hide under covers
no it can't be
surely witches aren't real
at dawn the sun
bids goodbye to the moon
paints the sky with the promise
of a perfect spring day

the cat flap swings
soft pads climb the stairs
kitten leaps onto my pillow
I want my breakfast
get up right now!
I pluck a cobweb from his soft
silky fur
where have you been
you curious boy?
he purrs and nuzzles close to my heart—
then
…just for a moment his green eyes flash red

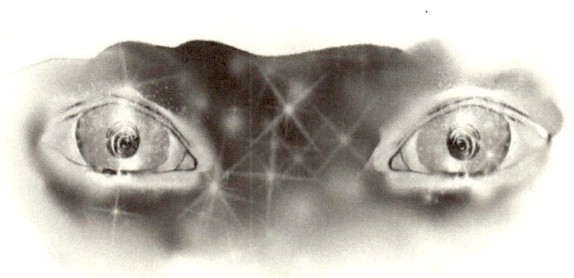

The Old School Murder Mystery
By Michael Noonan

Always, a smart, well-heeled place, where the fatal deed is
   done.
A five star hotel, a luxury liner, a private club,
Or some spotless, patrician mansion, with ivy clad walls
And lush, manicured grounds.
No self-respecting corpse
Would be seen dead in any lesser habitation.
As if to complement its classy setting,
The murder is invariably a clean, clinical job.
There is no messy, mutilated corpse, or blood splattered
   suit,
Here, where even death must show some dignity and
   decorum.
All is accomplished by a neat stiletto thrust,
Or phial of poison, or a well-aimed pistol shot.
And, as if some kind of justice is also done,
The victim is, without exception, a nasty piece of work.
A moody and malign misanthrope
Who did the dirt on everyone he knew.
There is no shortage of suspects in such a case.
The body is discovered and the household is alerted.
There is shock and alarm at the news of his death,
And the labyrinthine house is abuzz with rumour and
   speculation.
But no one is entirely surprised about that fatal deed.
As if the murder of such a person was not entirely
   unexpected.
'He only got what was coming to him',

Whispers one servant to another.
The tremulous butler rings up the Yard.
A photographer, pathologist and forensic team arrive
To examine the body and pore over the scene of the crime.
Then at length a dry, pedantic Inspector calls,
With a plodding, pedestrian assistant at heel.
The pathologist establishes the time and means of death,
And the investigation begins.
The two policemen study photos of the corpse,
Then question, in turn, each inhabitant of the house.
No one admits to having witnessed the fatal deed,
And all protest their innocence of the crime.
Unbeknown to the hapless and benighted officers
A cunning trap has already been laid,
To sabotage and undermine their investigation.
Unwittingly they stumble onto every false scent, red herring
And thread of stitched up evidence
That had been sinuously planted and arranged,
To slant and skew the case.
While the wary assassin, the author of the crime, and the
  deception,
Makes a demonstrative show of cooperating with the police,
And is deemed a useful witness.
His efforts reach their grim fruition.
A framed up fall guy, the witless victim of his doctored
  clues
And whispered suspicions,
Is taken, from the arms of a tearful spouse,
To the Station for further questioning.
He protects his innocence, but is charged with murder.
The evidence seems irrefutable.
An open and shut case, the press concludes.
In desperation his family hire the services of a legendary

sleuth,
To reopen the investigation.
He arrives at the mansion in his vintage car.
He's an upper class amateur of genius
With a double-barrelled name and cut glass voice.
A bon vivant, with exquisite manners and immaculate attire.
He comes from one of the better families,
Got a First at Oxford;
Is an excellent batsman, and a legend on the Polo field.
And his peerless reputation envelops him like an aura.
He comes with his doting, dog-like, devoted companion,
Who accompanies him on all his enquiries.
In order to wonder anew at each brilliant investigation,
And then chronicle and immortalise his legendary deeds.
He examines the murder scene,
Asks cryptic and mysterious questions;
Then recreates the circumstances of the crime.
He casually chews the stem of his pipe
And filters all the multifarious and convoluted facts
Through his prodigious brain.
He effortlessly outsmarts the dumb professional cops,
Sees quite through the planted evidence
And the camouflage of a fabricated alibi.
And then a conclusive motive is established
To clinch and close the case.
At length he corners the sly, sinuous villain—
His mask quite fallen, his confidence gone—
And makes him tearfully admit his guilt.
A man who only failed to execute the perfect crime
Through the arrival of the perfect detective.
The smooth, symmetrical investigation
Unfolds to an exquisite denouement.
Each loose end is tied,

Each enigma is neatly resolved.
The murderer is arrested and taken away,
The innocent dupe is released to the light of day,
The tainted victim is buried, and the great detective
Burnishes anew his unsullied reputation.
Everything is resolved
And calm, unruffled normality
Returns to the upper class abode.

Whodunnit?

By Cathy Bryant

Who killed the rich man?
Was it his wife
—poisoned his self-tan
to end his life?
Who killed the rich boss?
His deputy?
A quick push, then tossed
in machinery?
Who killed the rich dad?
Not his daughter?
Did the lamb take the bad
man to slaughter?
The talk of the town!
Was it the cat?
Yes! It tripped him on
the stairs, just like that.

Who Put the Cat Out?

By Shobana Gomes

Silence! Strange, not even a beep to raise awareness to
the sound of the electric kettle, done with boiling the
water—maybe for coffee or a splash of tea!
The kitchenette is quiet as a mouse, where is the Cat?

I walk into the living room, my steps silent as I tread
the floors, my slippers—soft, cushioned.
My eyes scanning, searching, berating my fear for the
unknown.
Why did fear find itself into my feelings of curious
probing? Unnerving!

The couch had furs stuck to its fabric, a depression
evident from the constant weight of animal reign on
it. Empty, the tell-tale sign of the missing Cat, so
glaring.

Accustomed was I, to the gentle morning cuddles from
the furry feline.
I sit on the couch, stilling my thoughts for a moment,
scanning for a sign of the cat's presence. I call out
softly—"Kitty, Kitty, come here baby. Where are
you?"

The silence deafens!
Hadn't I gently laid it to sleep the night before, not
before, padlocking the doors, shutting out the gust of
night breeze through windows that would have frozen
my Cat. Hadn't I?

The questions, a jumble of thoughts.

Where was Kitty? To traipse out of her comfort zone,
  was unbecoming, of her, of her plain kitty courage.

I get up from the couch. Louder my voice rings this
  time, "Kitty, here Kitty," I hear myself call out!
An eerie call to awakening, I hear my Cat, outside my
  door!

Meow, Meow, Meeee...0wwww, it went on...and on...
I hear you, Mistress, here I am,
Out in the cold,
Led by a hand,
That dealt with stealthy shows and wicked gleams,
Of sorcerer's guile.
I was led out in the night,
By the magic of the wizards,
Who retrieves from cats, their souls, and lives!
Nine in all, and live with each of it, as their own

Now,
My mistress walks with questions on her mind.

Who put the Cat out? It wasn't I! Not ever I!
Confused, I open the door in warm welcome,
Kitty jumps into my arms,
Happy and contented,
Back home with its Mistress.

Who put the Cat out? Kitty would know!
And I?
I was left with a confused mind, a steadfast heart, to

keep her safer than before.

Kitty said something in its baby feline language, I know not what!

Riddle Indeed

By Caroline Hurley

Last year, Uncle Pat died in Cairo
in circumstances yet unknown.
He did leave a will
but the nub was a riddle,
about where his house deeds were stored.

His whereabouts kept people guessing:
one week, Spain, next Brazil, then Hong Kong.
He sent home postcards
with no hint of those parties
he attended with state heads and kings.

"Below JP, dear Bob, and JFK,
locate Mustela Erminea
between Phasianus
Colchicus and Janus.
There the Holy Ones keep titles safe."

Such were the only directions
inserted for family guidance
about the hiding place
of Pat's mansion's mortgage
leading my dad, Bob a merry dance.

These brothers lived so far apart,
one a married man, one bachelor,
that rarely they bothered
to meet one another

so to Pat's house, Dad was a stranger.

"We'll have to get keys from the lawyer,"
Dad decided, "and go take a gander."
Without further ado,
I booked a choo-choo.
The address proved easy to discover.

In we went with our enigmatic verse.
It was I who saw JFK first.
"Look, Dad! US President!
And John Paul the Second!"
On the study wall hung the two pictures.

Then Dad copped the Latin cryptogram.
A stuffed pheasant, stoat, and speculum,
perched on a reference:
The Lives of The Saints.
There inside were the deeds. Solved problem!

Carnival
By Alex Kashko

A single discarded shoe and a bunch of flowers, a
  mystery
a dedication, a sacrifice to the lord of foolishness?
will stay before his statue till the end of never.
On the 30th of February his hammer
starts the time of misrule, the carnival
of fools, when it hits the bell.

The showman-priest taps the bell
Not meditating on the mystery,
of Carnival
nor the wise minds foolishness.
The sound of the hammer
on the bell resounds till the last day of never
when the flying purple pigs of never
dethrone the slaughter house king, break his bell,
smite the killjoy priests with the hammer
that releases the joy of their mystery
the frenetic freedom of foolishness
the wild dung flinging carnival

of fools, wise fools who use the carnival
to seek the boundaries of never,
and tread the line between wisdom and foolishness.
At the bottom of the sea a great brass bell
tolls a sunken mystery
in a city destroyed by a hammer.

The sacred healing hammer

bludgeons reason into submission letting carnival
become a sacred mystery
that the educated can never
fathom till the bell
chimes and they see the wisdom of foolishness.

Adults say only children may enjoy foolishness
Grown ups must work when the master's hammer
strikes the time clock bell
Splitting the carnival
from the world, never to reveal its mystery.
The temple and the carnival bell unleash foolishness
that hides a mystery unlocked by a hammer
that starts a carnival to calm the mind till the end of
  never

Mystery of the Quantum Skeleton

By Alex Kashko

He's been dead for some time
said the doctor compounding the mystery.
I wonder why he kept a skeleton
on the wall. When he was alive
he was the expert on quantum
worlds and lurked, a phantom
at conferences where the phantom
of the greats hovered all the time:
discrete explorers of quantum
worlds and the mystery
that in some worlds they were alive
and he was a talking skeleton

Make no bones about it, said the skeleton
I am no phantom
I am more alive
than those who are trapped by time
and sealed in the mystery
of the mischievous quantum
world where a quantum
of energy can become a skeleton
talking of an eternal mystery
in the pallid phantom
of serial linear time
in which we are all "alive"

The expert is no longer alive

to teach us a quantum
more about time
Soon he will be a skeleton
and perhaps a phantom
a perpetual mystery
for ghost hunters and a mystery
denied by sceptics while they are alive
a mystery solved when they enter the phantom
zone and become a quantum
dancing, a skeleton
immune to time

Well, said the phantom, it's no mystery how I spent
my time when I was alive:
I died of fluctuations in the quantum, left my doctor
my skeleton.

A Puzzling Crossing

By Janet Turner

Look to the tide timetables
to gauge the direction of flow.
Calculate currents and swell.

Ask the hairy ferryman what he heard
on the pink ferry's battered bridge
as it crossed the broad river mouth.

Question the woolly-hatted youth
in the pink ferry booth.
What did he see as he gossiped?

Get the passengers recounting
their tales. What did anyone see?
What was used and how was it done?

And whether he did it or not, someone
must answer for what has been done.
For it *will* be found out.

Whitby
By David Dixon

There's something fishy about Whitby,
And I don't mean the whiff of codfish,
Oh, it's fine with a fish and chip supper,
But strange in an autumn mist.
A feeling if you took the wrong turning
could run in with 'Barguest' the black dog
Or ahead where your vision is blurring,
A vampire lurks in the swirl of the fog.
There's something odd about Whitby,
I don't mean on a fair evening in June,
More when a northerly gale is running,
On a midwinter's night in half moon.
On the river a boat lie's waiting;
She's a three masted barque from the east,
On her stern is the name 'Demeter,'
Her figurehead is a blood sucking beast.
Aye it's a curious place that Whitby,
All cobbled streets and little shops,
Those snickets that lead to old taverns,
A Dickens town that time forgot.
Climb the stairs to St Mary's Chapel;
Amongst the tombstones of the blessed,
Read the names of the departed,
Some say here lie's the 'Count of Death.'
There's something not right about Whitby,
Like a distorted view through old glass,
Could be something to do with the lighting,
A morphing tween present and past.
Let the severed 'Hand of Glory;'

Lead you to the 'Masters' lair,
In the ruined Gothic abbey,
You will find the entrance there.
It's a funny old town that Whitby,
And I don't mean in a humorous way,
Painted on smiles in the china dolls parlour,
Does not mask what they convey.
Are they bewitched and locked in slumber?
Such full lips and rosy cheeks,
Could it be my imagination?
Or do I see the points of eye teeth.
There's something amiss in Whitby,
A slight feeling of menace, unease,
Times when you get the sensation,
Not all is as well as it seems.
When footsteps reveal behind you;
A man dressed in top hat and tails,
Tapping in stride on the pavement,
With a silver topped walking cane.
Dark secrets lay hidden in Whitby,
Lips sealed by the 'Wickerman's Oath,'
Passed down through each generation,
The vow of silence 'Under the Rose.'
Holding hands in the baker's shop window;
Cooked in the ovens of Hell,
Dusted with fine icing sugar,
Look! Twelve sabre toothed gingerbread men.

Eye to Eye
By Hannah Lashyro

It is an unwelcome sensation, the
rippling crawling uncertain
feeling tearing its way up my spine

Blinking, the clock blinks back at me
3:00 AM.

I face it eye to eye.
3:01 AM.

The silence blankets my bed room
it is molasses, suffocating my throat
whispering in my ear to *turnaroundturnaround*

As a tree is rooted to the ground I am
entrenched in my blankets and sweat
My arms and my nerves are hot and cold

I cannot face it behind me eye to eye
It has no eyes it has no name
I do not know its face
Piercing my chest all I know myself
is that I must
absolutely not
turn around.

He Promised Me a Rose Garden

By Helene Bowen

"I didn't do it!"

"But you had many motives, didn't you?"

"I sure did, but, I did not do it!"

The tall, good looking police officer, David Strong,
stared directly into my eyes for too long.
He spent time looking at my art work,
photos, and paintings on the walls.
The gloomy sequence of these visuals had become
shaded,
as the rooms had grown like *darker stalls!*

"It sounds like you did have some motives,"
he said as he turned to leave,
and I was left with the thought,
"What does he have up his sleeve?"

Neighbors were, no doubt, wondering
about what was going on!
With all the branches and uprooted trees,
and bushes strewn all around,
it looked as though a *tornado* had hit
only My very own ground!

One of the several things I liked about Brad was that
he promised me a rose garden.
But, the bushes grew taller than windows,

blocking my vision, without any pardon.
They had become the ***rose bushes from hell!***
The police returned, this time with a *warrant!*
Seems there's a lot *more* to tell.
"Yesterday's visit was about the vandalism of your yard.
Today, we have a report of a missing person....
your husband! We are seriously on guard!"

His sister reported him missing, insisting that I had killed Brad,
and that it was I who vandalized it, and chopped down my own yard!

Brad and I had had words of a torrent,
and now, alas, he was gone!
I could see through windows! Didn't worry 'til now,
but, police were *still searching, right down by the pond!*

Their questions were shocking and
really caused me to frown,
"Did he leave on his own?"
Or, did I put him in ground?
I was nervously getting mad,
but I was sure that
they knew that I hadn't harmed Brad!

When Brad returned after being sought after,
he contacted the cops, and
chuckled with nervous laughter,
as he laid out his tale of woe......

"I was disgusted with weedy gardens,
so many things to fix, and so, ***and so***,......."

He chopped down all the "damn rose bushes,"
all of the seeds he had sown.
He took off without notice,
and ran away from home!

Something Moved in the Conifer

By Luke Pinson

Something moved.
Maybe not.
Something moved. Within conifer.
Something moved again.
Let's go see.
Stretch.
Focus. Take path.
Closer now. Sit down.
Something is definitely in there; can hear it.
Let's cross grass. Slowly.
Slowly, slowly, pause! Something is there.
Slowly, slowly, slowly…
Something is in conifer, just above my head.
Something is moving very close to my head.
Get ready.
Get ready.
Get…
Something is moving away.
Something is on other side of conifer.
Something is getting quieter.
Relax. Sit down.
Something is not moving.
Can't hear anything.
Something has gone.
Yawn.
Check distance from house.
Focus on conifer.

Murder by Moonlight

By Angelica Esquivel

She enters the apartment in silence, slinks like a cat
through the dark
as her ill-adjusted eyes scan for evidence
regarding her boss's disappearance. A patch of light

from the table lamp casts shadows across her face.
The desk is covered with tax forms held down by glass
paperweights. She tugs on the handle of one of the
desk drawers.

It's locked. She pulls a bobby pin from her hair,
fiddles with the lock until she hears a faint *click*.

The drawer slides open and her eyes widen.
She quickly swipes the contents of the drawer,
stuffs them into the pocket of her black trench coat.
She turns, notices that the window is open,
the curtain blowing outward in the breeze.
Moonlight reflects off another pair of eyes,
glass figures in the night.

The Larcener

By Temilade Adetona

A crouching shadow burgeoned on the face of the
  street,
The eerie silence soared even to the deafening of ears,

Out of the blue was a scream, an ocean in this desert of
  quietude.

The larcener had again cast his swift fingers,
One as slippery as lye, hidden as night.

Two a night he sojourns, one edifice to the next,
A faceless pilferer of vast aptitude.

Ahead of the rise of dark his gaze had rested on all
  save Lucy and I,
Now her scream echoed through the serenity of
  nightfall.

A crouching shadow burgeoned on the walls of my
  home.

Pie Anyone?
By Stephanie Malone

I had a pie. Where did it go?
Who stole it? I want to know.
Was it the guy on the bench licking his fingers?
Or the lady that smells of apple which lingers.
Was it the toddler with crumbs around his lips?
Could it be the dog whose tail whips?
No! Its grandma enjoying my pie as I look on
Granny, can I have a piece before it is gone?

Who Saw Jane?

By Rosemary Yvery

Sometimes I play with sand
But she tells me to burn the castles
And when no one is looking around
She buries me whiles the wind whistles

Sometimes I play with dolls
Last night she made me burn them all
And I told mom
She said I'm too old for imaginary friends anymore

But I swear I see Jane in the mirror
When it's cracked and broken
Like my second grade teacher's voice when she's
singing tenor
Still mom says it's all in my head

Today Jane told me to turn off the lights
So my room looked like the night sky
Then she told me I'm her shadow
And shadows don't exist when there's no light

So we ended it there.

A Pillar's Destiny

By Adam Borzik

Intense drumming of drummers, followed by clapping
of clappers: tirelessly crawling and calling near the sea.

Here the dexterous detective holding his hollow hat,
Exploring the royal ruins; where once seamen stood so
  stiffly.
While the water and sand forced them to hide like a
  ragged rat.

The calls of ravished ravens on pillars, big as a flat.
A sergeant old and cold studies his gigantic glyphs
  gloomy
The two in dark dungeons discuss doodles, alongside a
  cat.

What did
The brick
See sergeant?
Poor passing.
Hands handing.
Bricks breaking.
Lavished lying.
Hammers hitting.
Nails nailing.
Herbs healing.
Cats clawing calmly,
At milk-mouthed mice, mostly.
But mighty mice may mount their mountains,
In due time. In another time, in an old time, as well as

in this time.

Halt was what he was called, when waves touched the baby's forehead.

He dreamt of fruits fresh, of skies stunning, of begonias blooming, in due time.

He had heroic friends fair, forgiving, fearless. Former farmers and tradesmen tough.

A tall man with a strong solid bow. A short man who polished his arrows, guarded by a skinny woman hiding in the shadows, with little cookie doughs.

The landlord's lavishes laid on his shoulders. The landlord's legs stood on many great lands.

Coming down like cats and dogs, one day, the crows yelled at vultures and mockingbirds.

The spires started shaking, cracks cracked, small stones started spinning, razors raddled,

Grand golden goblets getting grim, greasy, like the powerful posters purchased with pounds proudly,

When waves watered, the soil spicy, even sand sentinels slipped and abandoned posts.

Columns collapsing as the titan's legs grow tired,

A canvas of countless cubes, each falling off like frozen thawing ice cycles melting in the summer heat.

Children chasing roaches, Halt with their parents praying heavily; depressingly, hopelessly, desperately.

Suddenly the brave bows, and amazing arrowheads ascend,

Poseidon's palm ports, as the Gods hand out their dice, however this game this gamble is a flute no loot, played by two.

A hollow helpless hand reaches out! The detectives
dismay:
Two tigers, big and small, and a baker's baking beetle;
blessed.
The sergeant thinks thoroughly, near the tents ashtray.

The little towers, the lightless torches: Dust away!
Dust away!
As the serge scraps some stains from soggy stones:
Scrap away! Scrap away!
The two questioned calmly and quickly: Never
confessed! Never confessed!
When finally the investigative eye progressed, holding
a cookie jar, gray.

Intense drumming of drummers, followed by clapping
of clappers: Tirelessly crawling and calling near the
sea.

Knock
By Alan Miguel da Silva

A candle illuminating my sight
My heart heavy with the lies
Alone, for the first time I heard:
Knock knock
I did not ask, "Who is there?"

My knees were about to bleed
My throat was sore from crying
A veil covering bruises in my face
I prayed for salvation and heard it again:
Knock knock knock

I got up and dried my tears
My pounding chest exposing my fear
Demanding action, it insisted:
Knockknockknockknockknockknock
In panic, I held my breath

Aggressively the sound repeated itself
Harder, faster, begging me for help
Afraid of what was to come
I stood there ecstatic

Knock... Knock... knock...
Slower and erratic

Then, only silence and my modest smile
No more noises from the cemetery's undergrounds

He would never again knock me out
Our marriage was on the rocks,
May you forever rest trapped under them
Farewell, dear husband, who I buried like a gem

A Precious Item

By Rowan Gemma

Grains of sand scattered across the cement
A magnifying glass approaches
But no signs of the shiny object
Which has fallen from the poor man's finger

A hoot, a holler,
The man cries for help,
Devastated
Clueless of how it could've fallen
But it's his wedding ring

Spiked anxiety,
Emotional trauma
All comes to a halt
As relief washes over him

His eyes shift to his ring finger
And his ring is still there
Just as it was
And he questions the state of his imagination
But what made him hallucinate?
The ring is as shiny as his skin

Innocent My Foot!
By Tooni Oguntula

Harsh shouts and clanking glasses
merge to form discordant melodies,
wreaking havoc on my unfortunate eardrums,
and making my soul lash out in disgust.
Intently, I watch—
my eyes, swirling pools of amusement—
as the young bloke dances away
what's probably left of his sanity.
Wily fellow the bloke is,
casting subtle glances around every now and again
as he keeps up his act
of letting his soul go on the dance floor.
Delectably, the dried-up crimson on his worn-out sneakers
glistens under the gleaming, twirling ball.
A bloodied handkerchief peeking out
of his back pocket for fresh air.
Warily I watch as he steps out
from the over-bearing crowd,
glancing around one last time,
his eyes passing over my hooded frame as he takes his
leave.
Taking that as my cue,
I follow his slightly intoxicated form,
as one with the night,
to the alleyway next to a gas-station.
Hidden safely by a nearby vehicle,
I watch as he emerges from the alleyway,
a different shirt donning his torso,
along with a wrinkled, raggedy apron.

I keep my eyes solely trained on him
as he walks into the convenience store near the station.
If my hunches are correct,
he'll be awaiting his next victim.
A young lady hurriedly rushes into the store.
Suddenly, I hope my hunches
had taken a wrong turn, only for me
to witness the store blend in with night.

Shocked by the sudden occurrence, I start moving
towards the scene, calling for back-up from all near stations.
As soon as I am done, I hear a shrill scream
that is abruptly cut off.
Breaking out into a sprint,
I burst into the store and run
towards the only source of light,
streaming out from the back room.
Hurrying in, the gory sight before me
has me swaying on my feet.
His head snaps to mine and
he regards me with wide eyes and a scowl.
Innocent until proven guilty my foot!
Snarling, he tries to escape,
but easily, I hold down his scrawny frame,
and next thing I know, a piercing gunshot is heard.

Testimony: Murder Is My Prime Game

By Tooni Oguntula

Melancholia spreads through my system.
Utter despair fills me, in his presence, to the utmost
plateau.
Reluctantly so, I still accepted his apology offer;
Decidedly, I was convinced he had changed.

Eerie was the atmosphere in the house,
Right when I got back from the bar.
Instinctively, I grabbed the nearest thing—an empty
bottle of Martini.
Stalking past the overly-quiet birds,
My heart rate increasing to the maximum;
Yelling out his detestable name, only to get no reply.
Pushing myself as I got to the last step,
Rancid odors nearly ran me over.
Immediately I ran to open up the bowl of potpourri.
Marching over to the closet in the bedroom,
Endeavoring to stay calm, I could only blanch at the
sight of his gruesome figure.
Giving up my resolve, I ran out to my neighbor's
house gasping.
Angst setting in, I rushed to reel in my hysteria.
Minutes later, the police showed up and the
paramedics took him. .Exhaling deeply, I was
comforted, but only for a while.

Pocketknife

By Audrey Xuan

Evidence boxes sit on shelves
Rows upon rows of shelves
Each one carrying a few items
A lock of golden hair—from a kind young woman who
was just admitted to Stanford
A cheap polyester necktie—from a disillusioned man
who had two degrees but no job
A creased Polaroid of a boy—from a loving mother
who was taken too soon
In one box,
There's nothing but a pocket knife
The creamy white handle still spattered with maroon
specks of blood
Indistinguishable from the rust that has built up over
time
As year upon year passed, the crime staying unsolved
Until one day the box was just tucked away in the
back,
Never to be seen of,
Never to be thought of,
Ever again.
This was not the murder weapon.
A young man, bright-eyed and gentle, carved his
initials into a tree with this knife, along with a
message:
"I was here today. I'll see you tomorrow."